The
Betrayed Prince

JESSICA NELSON

Cover Design by:
Sweet & Spicy Designs

Paperback-Press
an imprint of A & S Publishing
A & S Holmes, Inc.

ISBN-10: 1-945669-29-2
ISBN-13: 978-1-945669-29-3
:

ACKNOWLEDGMENTS

I'd like to acknowledge my mother, who got me to start writing; my husband and two children, for putting up with my hours of absence while I wrote this story. I couldn't have done this without my amazing family standing behind me.

Sharon Kizziah-Holmes with Paperback-Press, your help in getting this book published will always be appreciated.

Last but not least, thanks to Jaycee DeLorenzo at Sweet and Spicy Designs for the awesome cover art.

CHAPTER 1

"Man, this is the most amazing site I have ever seen. I can't believe you didn't tell me you lived here sooner."

"HAHA, you wouldn't have believed me if I told you so I just showed you, but this is not the only thing I want to share with you. I have kept this from you and everybody I know and it has been killing me keeping it from you, Damon. I just hope you still accept me in your life after I show you the biggest secret of my life and my family's lives as well; but I wish for you to know the pack and that you are friends with a wolf who has staked claim to the love of his life which is you."

"Hold on a second Derek. Did I hear you just say, staked a claim to the love of your life which is me?

"Yes, you did hear me say that and I can tell it is a shock to you"

"You damn right it's a shock to me. I hope to

hell you're joking about it because you know I don't swing that way and I know you don't as well. We both have girlfriends and we both slept with girls."

"No, Damon, I didn't sleep with the girls I dated. I only told you I did so you wouldn't find out I was in love with you and so I wouldn't lose having you in my life."

"Damon, Damon. Come on man wake up we gotta go. The girls are waiting on us."

"Derek, holy shit man I had the strangest dream."

"You can tell me about it after we get back. The girls really want to go out to eat and see a movie."

"You mean they want a double date with each other? But, I thought they told us they don't do double dates because they are lame."

"You got me there, but they are here breathing down my neck to wake you up and go out together or something. So get up man, I can't handle two women on my own. They are overpowering me."

"I can't believe you're telling me two women overpower the mighty wolf Derek. That can't be true."

"Why did you call me the mighty wolf Derek? What exactly was that dream you were having, Damon?"

"Are you guys going to come out with us or not? We really want to go out with you guys now!" yelled Molly

Damon got up and walked out of his bedroom in nothing but pants and says to both girls,

"Fuck no we are not going out with you girls tonight. We want to have some guy time and less bitching because things don't go your way. So there is the door and we will see you both later."

Molly's jaw drops and Kate takes a breath before saying, "Are you both really turning us down? I can't believe what I am hearing. You guys always want to go out and have guy time. Where is the 'us' time and the friends together time? Don't we get to have a chance to be with you both at one time or even go out to eat or then the movies?"

Derek walked in with a look of bewilderment on his face before looking at the girls and tells Kate they are over and he wants her to leave. He turns to Molly and says he can't speak for Damon but he wants her out to. As the girls leave Molly hears Damon say that the two of them were over as well because he can't take the mood swings any longer and he is sorry.

Derek walked over to the couch and sat down looking at Damon and tells him to explain why he called him mighty wolf Derek.

"Come on man it was just a dream. Why do you want to know so bag?"

"Because I want to know how in the world you know that I am a wolf."

"I might still be dreaming if you say you really are a wolf and that we both just dumped our girlfriends at the same time and for the same reasons."

"No man you're not dreaming, you're wide awake and in the living room with me and we are both talking about me being a wolf and yes we both just dumped our girlfriends at the same time and for the same reasons. Now tell me how the fuck you know I am a wolf."

"I don't know man. All I know is that I had a dream about us in the mountains in a really big house and you telling me you want to share yours and your family's secret with me about you being a wolf and you wanting me to accept you as yourself fully; that you have staked a claim to the one you love which is me. Then you wake me up to deal with the girls. Then we both dump them and now we are talking about my dream. So there, now we're all caught up and now I am going back to bed because I feel like shit."

"Feel like shit how? Because you dumped your girlfriend or because of me or are you getting sick?"

"I feel like I am getting sick. I don't care about the girlfriend thing right now and well, you are who you are and I will always accept you. No I am going back to bed. Goodnight Derek."

Before Damon could move, Derek was right in front of him. The look in his eyes was happiness and the next thing Damon knew is he is getting crushed in a bear hug from his friend. "Derek, you're crushing me. I can't breathe."

"Shit, I am sorry. I am just really happy you accept all of me and you won't leave me. I am very grateful, Damon."

"Alright man I will see you when I wake up again. Night, Derek."

"Night, Damon"

As Damon lies down, Derek is still wondering about what his friend had dreamed about what he did. He needed questions answered and the only way to get them answered was to go to the mountain home his friend dreamed about. So he called his mother to let her know he and Damon will be coming to see them and he needed some answers about what is going on.

Derek started packing both of their things while Damon is sleeping. He decided he will let Damon sleep the whole trip there so he won't have to do anything but wake up in the place he dreamt of. He went to the kitchen and grabbed a cup and fills it with water and grabs medicine for Damon and takes it to him.

"Damon, I brought you something that will help you sleep better and will help with your cold if you have one."

"Thanks man," was all Damon could say because after he took the pills Derek gave him, he was out cold which puts a smile on Derek's face because he knew Damon wouldn't wake up till tomorrow afternoon, but he still waited a bit longer before finishing up with the packing to make sure Damon was sleeping soundly.

When he was satisfied he went on packing. When Derek finished with the packing, he loaded everything he packed for the both of them in his car and laid the front seat down and put a blanket over the seat and a pillow at the top for Damon to sleep comfortably there. After he had got it ready, he went back into the house and carried Damon to the car and buckled him in the seat, covered him with another blanket then closed the door. He went back up and locked up the apartment and returned to his car to leave but he was halted by a car pulling up. When he saw the girls in the window he got into his car and started it to leave. He began to back out of his spot when the girls blocked his exit.

Derek got out of his car and told them to move out of the way because they were going on a trip and don't have time to mess around with crying babies that can't get over the fact they have been dumped.

Kate got out of her car and walked right up to Derek and was about to slap him when the both looked over and saw that Damon had got out of the car and was walking right for them. He looked right at Kate and then at Molly who was still in Kate's car, but what he said next shocked Derek even more than before.

"Kate, if you and Molly don't get the fuck away from here you both will cause something to happen that we all will regret in the end. Now as you can see you both have really pissed off Derek to the point of shaking like crazy. I can practically hear his anger in my ears and I am telling you both to get the fuck away from us and do not bother us again. Or I will have no choice but to call the cops and tell them mine and my roommate's ex-girlfriends will not take a hint and leave us alone," Damon said

"You would really do that to us after being together for a year and a half?" Molly asked Damon

"You damn right I will. Now fucking leave us alone. We are trying to leave and you are blocking our way and causing a scene in front of our apartment. Now fucking let us go so we can go on our trip to see Derek's parents."

The anger on Derek's face had been replaced with what the fuck how did he know. Derek saw movement out of the corner of his eye and ducked just as a hand was coming towards him but then he heard skin hitting skin and looked just as Kate's hand moved towards her face in shock. "Why did you do that? Why did you block me from hitting Derek?"

"Because he doesn't deserve to be hit just like I don't deserve it. You both wanted so much from us and you bitched when nothing went your way and both of us has had enough of it. We don't deserve it so we broke up with you both and now we want you to leave us alone but you can't even do that so we decided to take a trip to see Derek's family. Then we are going to see mine and no we didn't take you guys to meet them because we didn't want to. Now we are going to leave and so are you guys."

"Do you guys really want it to be this way? We can't even come talk to you about changing anything? It's just the end?" Molly asked from Kate's car

"Yes it is just the end, nothing more nothing less. Now leave so we can," Derek replied

Derek and Damon got back into the car as Kate got into hers to leave. Once the girls left the guys began their journey to the mountains. As soon as they got onto the highway, Derek was about to ask how the fuck Damon knew where they were going but when he looked over at his friend he saw that Damon was already back asleep.

Without even realizing what he was doing Derek grabbed hold of Damon's hand as he drove down the road but what really got him was he could almost hear Damon in his mind. That shocked him well enough to let go and focus on the drive at hand. He knew it was going to be a long trip so he decided he would drive for a while then look for a hotel to stay at; then get back on the road once Damon wakes up so he could find out just how he knew what was going on even before it could be explained to him.

Derek drove for the whole day and part of the night until he started getting tired. He pulled off the highway to look at the map for the closest hotel but sleepiness got the better of him.

When he woke up he felt like he was moving. When realization hit him that the car was moving he jumped up and hit his head on the roof of the car.

"Fuck," Derek yelled

"HAHA, easy man you'll break through the roof doing that."

"When did you take over driving and how long was I asleep?

"Well I took over yesterday morning around five am and you've been asleep since then."

"What time is it now?"

"Well it's almost midnight," Damon said while smiling

"Shit man I am sorry. I can take over driving and you can sleep. By the way, do you know where we are going and how to get there?"

"Yes I do man. You put everything in writing on the map," Damon replied while pulling off the road

When they got to the shoulder of the road, Derek took out the map. "Are you sure I wrote on this map?"

"Um, Damon, there is no writing on the map. It is just a map. Are you sure I wrote on this map?"

"That's not the right map, Derek. I was talking about the map in the back seat."

Derek reached for the map in question and was in complete shock. He remembered the map by all the wolf markings from when he left the mountains from long ago. He couldn't believe Damon could understand the writing on the map.

"Damon, you can understand this?"

"Yeah man, I don't know how but I do."

After that they both got out of the car and started to switch sides, they heard a roaring coming at them. Before they knew it at least a dozen bikers surrounded them. Derek shot to Damon's side as three bikers got off their bikes and started walking towards them.

"Well, well, well, if it isn't Derek Wolfram. Long time no see."

"Damon, stand back," Derek growled

"So this is the one you left for. He is really cute. Mind if I have a little chat with him?"

"No you may not have a chat with him. He is no concern to you. What do you want?"

"Nothing much, just a little payback."

After the biker said that, four bikers were on Derek the instant he finished speaking. Derek was held down while two of them grabbed Damon and took him to the biker who had gotten on his bike and waited for them to bring him Damon. They forced Damon on the bike and it started instantly.

"Now you can try to save him or you can stand back and watch him become mine."

After the final words were said from the biker, they took off before Damon could get off the bike. When they were a good distance away the other bikers started to show up. Damon started to feel so alone and worried about Derek so much that he started to actually cry for the first time in years.

The only thing he kept thinking was "please be okay Derek." As soon as he thought that, he got a slight buzzing that caused him to get a headache; then he heard Derek's voice saying he was going to find him and keep him safe.

Damon froze and closed his eyes. He felt like all of his energy had been drained from his body and he welcomed the empty void of sleep taking over.

"Fuck," was all he heard before going completely unconscious. Then he felt an arm wrap around him and move him in between a pair of arms. Then he felt movement again.

CHAPTER 2

When Damon woke up he felt really warm and dizzy. He tried to sit up.

"Easy, don't push yourself too much. You've got one hell of a fever and we can't break it with medication so we are trying to sweat it out of you."

"Who are you?"

"My name is Luka. What is your name?"

"Damon."

"It's nice to meet you, Damon. I am sorry about taking you away from Derek like that but, we were hired to do that.'

"What do you mean hired to take me?"

"We got a phone call from an unknown number a couple of days ago. They gave us the route you and Derek were taking and said we were to take you and wait to receive a call telling us were to drop you off and get the cash."

"So I am just a job for you so I can be taken to someone I don't even know. That sounds so lame."

"You have no idea about what is going on or why someone would hire us to take you?"

"I don't know a damn thing. I've been alone since I was five, other than having Derek around me. When I was old enough to know, my parents were killed and I had no other family. Derek stayed with me till you just split us up, so no I don't know anything."

Luka told Damon to rest some more then he'll be back to check on him again soon, then he left the room. Damon had no idea how he was going to fall asleep after hearing that but he soon fell back asleep.

He woke up to shouting in the other room. Damon got out of bed ignoring his weakened state. He wanted to know what was going on and he really had to use the bathroom, plus he wanted a hot shower. He opened the door.

"Luka? Are you here?" Damon asked outside the door.

"I am coming, Damon," Luka answered

Damon leaned against the door frame while he waited. He closed his eyes for just a second then jumped when he felt a hand on his cheek.

"You shouldn't be up, Damon. What do you need?"

"I really need to use the bathroom and I was hoping for a hot shower. I stink."

Luka laughed and said he can show me the way and I could take a shower while he gets a change of clothes for me.

Damon thanked him as he closed the bathroom door. When it was closed Damon started getting undressed and did his business, then turned on the shower for his long hot bath. When the shower was just the right temperature for him, he climbed in and started the process of washing himself off.

Once he was done he just stood there and let the hot water relax all of the tiredness out of his muscles. After a while of just standing there Damon decided it was time to get out, so he turned the water off and stepped out to get a towel. When he was finished drying off he heard a knock on the door. He opened it and saw Luka there with some clothes in his hands.

"Thank you, Luka" Damon said

"You're welcome. You are not a prisoner here so you can do whatever you like."

"Well I can't do anything but stay here till I am better, then after that I have to go to someone I don't even know. I might as well be a prisoner."

The next instant Damon felt arms wrap around him and pull him close to a hard chest. He didn't know what to do but stand there frozen.

"I am not going to harm, Damon. I just had the urge to hold you to comfort you. But, know this, I have strong feelings for you and I don't know why. I've never felt this for anybody in all my years."

"Luka, why is your body so cold?"

"Because, young one, I am a vampire and I have no body heat."

"No way vampires are real too? I only found out about Derek, what, three or four days ago," Damon said in a rush and collapsed against Luka while holding his head.

"Shit, you mean to say you had no idea of wolves or vampires or any super naturals out there? Don't you even know about yourself?" Luka said while keeping a firm hold on Damon.

"Damon, I am sorry about shouting. I know you are not well but you must know you are royalty."

"*What!?*"

"With that I now know you didn't."

"How was I supposed to know? I don't even know my past. All I know is what I told you already. Now please excuse me," Damon said in a broken voice

Damon stepped out of the bathroom and was just about back to his room when he got really weak and started to collapse when he felt arms wrap around him before he could hit the ground. Then he got pulled into a dream.

There was so much blood and so many bodies. There were dozens of people shouting and crying. Then a man came running up to me the grabbed me by the shoulders and then started running while saying I must save myself and run. Never look back. I continued to run straight into the woods when hands grabbed me and then there was a sharp pain in my neck.

Damon woke up with a jerk and jumped out of bed and started to run for safety but Luka was there to stop him and wrap him in his arms while he cried.

"Hush now, Damon, you're safe, you're safe." Luka told him

"There, there was so much b-blood and so many b-bodies, then a man told me to run, the next thing were arms grabbing me and then there was a sharp pain in my neck. I was so terrified. Then I woke up feeling the need to run away and now you are saying I am safe and comforting me," Damon said while crying

Luka only stood there and tightened his grip on Damon. Then the scent of fresh blood hit him and he pulled away and stared at the bite mark on Damon's neck. Before Luka realized it Damon had passed out and started to drop to the floor, but Luka had Damon up and in his arms in one swift movement.

As Luka carried Damon back to his room, he started to feel that not only do the people around Damon want to harm him but now his dreams are brought into the mix. Luka walked into the room and closed the door with his foot. He laid Damon down on the bed and watched as he slept. When Damon started to twitch, Luka grabbed his hand and noticed that Damon started to relax. When Damon rolled toward Luka's and his hands, Luka released his grasp and laid next to Damon and wrapped him up in his arms.

When Damon was completely relaxed, Luka's mind raced with so many thoughts he couldn't put words to and fell asleep while holding Damon.

When Luka woke up, Damon was gone. He shot up out of bed to go looking for him. When he opened the door Damon was on the other side. He had a towel wrapped around him as if he took a shower but didn't run away.

"I'm sorry if I woke you when I got up, but I wanted a shower," Damon told Luka.

But all Luka could think about was, why didn't he run? All of his men were asleep and nobody would have been able to stop him.

"Why are you looking at me like that?" Damon asked.

Instead of answering, Luka wrapped his arms around Damon and said, "I thought you had run away."

"I have no need to run away. I haven't been able to keep the images out of my mind; but last night when you touched me they all vanished and I don't understand why, so I want to find out," Damon answered

"You want to remain here? But, what about the one you vowed to return to and the one that you love?" Luka asked

"I'm sure he will understand if I explain everything to him, but he had kept much from me over the years so he'll be alright," Damon answered him

"Besides I have to find out if what he said is true and if what I feel is true or not, because what I'm battling with is a lot more complex than him proving he truly loves me," Damon added before Luka could respond.

Luka rushed to Damon and wrapped him in a tight hug and says. "Thank you for not leaving me and I also want to figure things out with you."

"Thank you, I guess, but I have to figure things out on my own for the most, part but maybe you could help me with the dreams and maybe explain what some of them may mean, and why I am starting to have the injuries on my body that I have in my dreams," Damon said.

"I'll try my best to help you with understanding your dreams the best I can and if I can't help then we can find someone who can. I have these feelings and I don't understand them at all, but I want to help and protect you anyway I can," Luka said.

After their talk Luka walked from the room so Damon could get dressed and so he could clear his head. Luka went to the garage to work on his bike and get it ready for the trip they have coming up. Luka thought long and hard on where they should go for answers. The place he came up with was a start and that was to find Damon's mom. He thought about asking Damon if he knew either of his parents but he couldn't bring himself to do it. Then it hit him. He could get a sample of blood from him and look in the data for them. That's when he put his plan into motion and went to Damon and asked him if he could change the bandages on his neck.

"Oh I had forgotten about these. Please go ahead." Damon answered

Luka said thank you and he changed the bandages. He took the others off and laid them on the nightstand, then he put ointment on the bite marks and put new bandages on.

"Thank you for remembering Luka. I really did forget about them."

"No need to thank me. I only wish to take care of you," Luka said

After he finished changing the bandages he picked up the two he had put on the nightstand and walked out again. He walked down the hall to the basement door and opened it. He went down the steps to where the lab is. He walked up to Jaxon, his right hand man, and handed him the bandages.

"Jaxon, I have a job for you to do. I need you to compare this blood to the others that are on file," Luka said.

"Ah, Luka, you do know that the only samples we have on file are supernaturals' right? And he is human," Jaxon said.

"There is something about him that is off; and yes I know that, Jaxon, but I still want you to check," Luka said as he left.

When Luka returned to the bedroom. He saw Damon lying on his side watching a movie. When Luka sat down on the bed next to him, he smiled. They stayed and watched a couple more movies then someone knocked on the door. When he opened the door he saw Jaxon with a very unsettling expression on his face.

"What is it, Jaxon?"

"Um, you're not going to believe this. Come with me," Jaxon said.

Luka looked back and saw that Damon was asleep and closed the door quietly.

"This better be good Jaxon. I shouldn't leave him when he sleeps. Something always happens to him so make it fast," Luka said irritatingly.

CHAPTER 3

When they got back to the lab Jaxon ran to the computer and turned the screen so Luka could see it. When Luka's eyes landed on the screen, he froze.

"Luka, man this boy is something else. He has every strand of super natural's code in his blood. There is no way to find his parents or find out where he came from," Jaxon says

Luka couldn't find the right way to ask his question but before he could even form the words, he and Jaxon heard someone screaming in pain. They both ran as fast as they could to Damon. When they got to the room, the others were there. They were holding Damon on the bed and all of them watched as designs started to show on his skin like tattoos. "What happened? Why are you holding him down?" Luka asked.

"H-he was throwing himself all over the room

cutting up his arms. Then he started floating so I got the others to help me hold him, down then this shit started showing up on his skin," Conrad answered

Luka walked over to the bed and laid his hand on Damon's bare chest and the thrashing stopped and Damon calmed down.

"Release him," Luka ordered.

"But what if it happens again?" Yuki asked.

"It won't, trust me. For some reason I can calm whatever is raging inside of him. We must protect him and not let anybody get to him. If we do we kill the only living royal blood line of all races of supernaturals." Luka told them.

There was a loud intake of breath from all of them.

"The only living royal blood line? You mean to tell us that he is the high prince of all of us supernaturals?" Sai asked

"Yes that is exactly what I am saying. We must protect the prince at all costs. We can't let him fall into the wrong hands. We must get him to the palace," Luka told his men.

"Sai, you are faster alone. Please take this to the palace and tell them we have found the prince and that we are bringing him home. Also add that he has chosen us six as his guards," Luka ordered.

"But why must I add sir."

"Because if you don't they will come for him and he will be in danger alone. Only the six of us know how to handle his episodes, nightmares, injuries or anything else that can go wrong with him," Luka answered.

"Yes, sir, I understand," Sai answered and got

ready to leave on his mission.

Before Sai got all the way out the door, Damon woke up.

"Who are you guys? Where is Luka?" Damon asked sacredly.

"I'm here, Damon, right here," Luka said as he sat on the bed.

"And, these men are Jaxson, Yuki, Sai, Conrad, and Sebastian. They are my most trusted friends and now the six of us are your loyal guards. We will keep you safe from harm," Luka added while holding Damon's hand

"I saw so many things. I don't think I can describe them all or put words to the images," Damon said confused.

He sat up on the bed and put his face in his hands as tears fell down his cheeks. The six men looked at each other in confusion then Luka moved behind Damon. Luka pulled Damon back onto his chest and wrapped his arms around him.

"Sai, you may leave now but be sure to call us daily and the rest of you begin packing. We are leaving tomorrow night," Luka said

"Yes, sir," they all said together

When they left Luka and Damon alone in the room, Damon began to relax in Luka's arms.

"You have no need to fear those men. They will protect you from anything that wants to harm you and so will I," Luka whispered.

"I'm so confused I don't know what to do. I want to stay and find out why I am the way I am but I want to run away and not look back. I want everything in my head to disappear. I don't want to fight my heart from keeping my feeling from overflowing when you're near or from breaking because of losing Derek. I want to be free from it all and not look back. I want it all to go away so I can be normal and not be afraid," Damon said in whispers.

All Luka could do was hold him close and say everything will be alright and that he wants to stay with him and protect him. Damon's breathing was shallow and his heart had a soothing beat. Luka moved to where they were both lying down. Luka kept Damon in his arms while they slept. Then Luka woke up to a strange sound outside. He carefully moved out of bed so he didn't wake Damon. When Luka opened the door Jaxon was walking towards him.

"Luka, there is movement outside all around the place and there are too many of them."

"Very well, I'll lock the door and we will all go after them. We must protect Damon." Luka replied.

He turned and locked the door that led to Damon and turned to his men as they all gathered before him.

"Let's go welcome our guest," Luka ordered as his eyes turned red.

As they got outside of the house they separated and went in all directions to attack the enemy. As the fighting began nobody noticed the single wolf that entered the house until it was too late. The fighting ended with all of them bound in silver chains. The wolf that entered the house came out with Damon in his arms.

"No don't take him please," Luka begged.

"You have no right to beg for him to stay when you took him from me to begin with. He was never yours to take," Derek growled.

Before Derek could react, Damon was out of his arms and on the ground screaming in pain with blue flames covering his body and burning his clothes, revealing the symbols that have begun to glow red.

"Luka! Luke, help me please!" Damon screamed

"Please release me so I can help my mate. Please I beg of you," Luka pled once more and began to get angry for them allowing Damon to remain in pain.

He watched as Derek dropped down next to Damon and reached out to touch him only to worsen the pain because Damon's cries for help got louder and he began to cry.

"Please, Luka! please help me! Save me! It Hurts so much!" Damon begged between screams.

Luka's rage boiled over as Damon's pleas for him got ignored. In the next moment all eyes were fixed on Luka as a bright glow emanated from him and his chains broke. Luka raced over to Damon and wrapped his arms around him as the blue flames coated his body. He began to talk soothingly to Damon and told him he was there and not letting go of him and he would always be there to save him from the pain and fear. All of the men watched as the flames began to die out and they saw Damon wrapped in Luka's arms crying heavily.

Luka's deadly gaze landed upon Derek. "Leave now and I shall not kill you for harming my mate."

As Luka finished speaking he raised his hand towards his men. The wolves all gasped as the chains binding them fell to the ground. The four of them rush to guard Luka and Damon from further harm. As the men encircled them, Damon raised his head off of Luka's chest and saw what was taking place around him.

"Derek, Derek, is that you?"

"Yes, Damon, it is me. I've been searching for you every day only to find you and cause you and your mate more pain with one touch. I only wanted to come and save you and take you where you could be safe," Derek replied.

Damon looked at Luka and then looked back to Derek. "What do you mean cause me more pain with one touch?"

"Damon, I touched you, carried you in my arms and then you were on the ground covered with blue flames, begging for the blood sucker to help and save you. I wanted to try and help you but your flames got bigger and caused you more pain,"

Damon flinched in fear from Derek shouting at him and hid his face in Luka's chest again as he began to shake in fear as the tears he held back fell. Luka started to growl and his eyes turned bright red.

"You should not yell at him and make him more afraid of what's happening than he already is. Do not shout at him because of your stupidity and the way you handle things. I will not sit here and let him be in any pain or be afraid. Leave now wolf and leave him in peace," Luka snapped.

Derek looked at Luka and then down at the fragile Damon. Let's go men. We can come find him again."

"What do you mean let them go? We should kill them and be done with it. We have wasted too much time hunting them down. Just because you wanted the boy," a pack member said

Before anyone could react, they all fell unconscious but the one thing they didn't expect was Damon coating all of them in blue flames and burning anyone who tried to touch them.

"How is he doing this? He is unconscious. How is he protecting them?"

"I don't know but we have to leave. Everyone is getting burnt when they approach," Derek answered.

The pack agreed to leave and find Damon again and take him before the others could make a move to stop them. Damon started to wake up as a bright light hit his eyelids. He sat up and saw he and the others were outside and the sun was coming up.

"Luka, Luka, Luka wake up its morning and you're all outside."

He moved to the others and tried to wake them but it was no use.

"Luka, please wake up. I can't move you all inside by myself….Please wake up," Damon continued to cry.

He looked up and saw that the sun had gotten higher and stood up to try and get them all inside. While light-headed and drained of energy, he grabbed Luka's arms and began to drag him towards the house. He had to pause to open the door and pull him the rest of the way inside. Damon went back out after he got Luka through the door. He grabbed onto Jaxon's arms and began to drag him to the house. Damon went back out to get the other three of them. He got beside Yuki and began to pull him towards the house. Damon kept losing energy but he kept pulling to get his friends inside safe from the sun. Damon had gotten three inside and had to go back for Conrad and Sebastian. Damon walked out and grabbed hold of Conrad's arms and pulled. He fell a couple times trying to get him to the house. As Damon got closer to the house he saw that the sun was getting closer to Sebastian.

Damon just about got Conrad inside when he saw that Luka was starting to wake up. He saw Luka slowly rise to his feet and walk out the door toward Sebastian. Damon finally got Conrad inside and saw that Luka had gotten Sebastian in as well. Damon went around to all the windows and blacked them out so the sun wouldn't hit anybody inside the house. Once all of that was done, Damon ran and got blood bags for all of them and watched Luka wake them all up and give them a bag so they could wake up more.

"Damon, Luka what the hell happened?" Jaxon asked.

"I woke up in the front yard with everyone around me. I tried to wake all of you up because the sun was coming up. But, when nobody woke up I dragged you guys inside. I'm sorry about the cuts and torn clothes." Damon answered exhausted.

"Do not apologize for our clothes and minor cuts. You saved our lives by pulling us inside. You're exhausted and yet you got us safely inside. You could have left us burn," Luka stated.

"Why would I......" Damon started to say but exhaustion won and he passed out.

Luka rushed to catch Damon before he hit the floor.

"Damon, are you alright?" Jaxon asked worried. He received no answer.

"Damon used so much energy. I saw what he had done for us. He protected us from the wolves by shielding us with flames and burning them as they tried to touch us. He kept us safe by pulling us inside the house as the sun rose. He could have let them kill us and go with them, yet he stayed with us and I don't understand why," Sebastian told them.

"Damon, is someone who won't turn his back on others. He would rather protect us because we have protected him," Jaxon said.

"Though you both make good points, neither of you are correct. Damon stays with us because he loves us. He protects us because he bears the marks of the vampire prince. He is our lord and master and he protects us because he feels it in his blood. Have you ever noticed every time there is danger or one of us is harmed he is always there for us no matter what? Damon will not run and he will not betray us" Luka stated boldly.

"We understand what you're saying Luka but how do we honestly know for sure he isn't just playing us and baiting us for the wolves? He only found out about all of this not that long ago. So why help people you trust or help keep us alive?" Yuki said angered.

"Because I choose to help and I chose to save you. I don't do things that would harm people. I live my own life and I do what I want. I have no need to bait you or betray you to the wolves. I do everything by choice," Damon said weakly.

"Damon, you shouldn't be up," Luka interjected.

"You can say that all you want and you can try to tell me many things but there is something I chose to do," Damon replied while looking at Yuki.

Luka and the others stared at each other.

"What exactly do you have to do?" asked Conrad.

"I will be leaving to go release Sai from Derek and the others," Damon said as he walked to the door.

As Damon opened the door and began walking down the sidewalk, he heard Luka yelling for him to come back and saying it's too dangerous for him to go alone. Damon continued to walk away and head towards the place he saw in his dreams. The place where Sai is located. While walking Damon tried to come up with ways to get Sai to safety. He could only think of one. even though it is daylight, he could wait for night to release him. His thinking came to a halt when he rounded the last corner and saw two wolves standing guard by a house. At his approach Damon asked them to get Derek and he would only speak to Derek. One stayed with Damon as the other ran inside to get Derek.

"Derek, Derek, that boy you call Damon is here and he said he would only talk to you," said Cole.

At that, Derek jumped to his feet and quickly went out to Damon. "Damon, how did you find this place? Have they been watching us to be able to attack us?" Derek asked angrily.

"Derek, if you think I am here to confirm or deny something about them, you are wrong. I am here of my own free will and I want you to release my friend tonight and before you ask, yes I would do the same if he was a wolf. I will not use one against the other, nor would I betray you or them, I want no blood shed. I ask this of you because I am the high prince of all supernaturals and because you are my friend and you know I don't lie about things. Now will you release my friend?" Damon said with great honesty and loyalty.

"So you were told who you are? And I know you wouldn't do that to us or them. I will release your friend on one condition. You will stay here with us and never return to them again," Derek said with jealousy

"Yes I found out who I am. You know I can order you to release him but I can't do that because I made a promise to myself and I'll see this all the way through. I don't fully understand what's happening to me or why it is but I need to understand. I am sorry but I can't stay with you. I have to get back to them. I am only here to ask you to release someone who is not part of this. They saved my life and they will always be there for me. Please, Derek, I don't want anybody hurt over me. So if you ever cared about me, you would either join with us and figure it all out or stay out of the way. I don't know how to control what is wrong with me or do I know how to stop it once it starts. I do know they can help me through it and I know you guys get hurt when you come near, so please release him and let us leave," Damon said.

Before Derek could respond, Damon dropped to the floor crying in pain and he heard the vampire screaming for Damon and begging to help him. Derek signaled for one of them to release the vampire and bring him to Damon.

CHAPTER 4

Damon's cries became screams as blue flames erupted from his body. Derek looked at his friend but was caught off guard as the vampire showed up and dropped to his knees beside him

"Damon, relax and take deep breaths. I'm going to take you out of here soon, I swear. Please bear with the pain. I know it hurts but I promise I'll help make it better. Please release me to help him. He won't last long if this isn't kept under control," Sai said looking at all of the wolves.

"Take him and tell the others this message. I will find a way to keep him from you guys and that you will never see him or be able to touch him again," Derek threatened.

Sai nodded his head then picked up Damon. Once Damon was in his arms the blue flame coated Sai and protected him from the sun light. Once he realized he wouldn't burn, he took off running towards the rest of them. He ran down the road without even staying out of public eye, but nobody seemed to notice two people covered in flames so he kept running. As soon as the house was in sight he yelled for them to open the door. As it came open Sai went inside and directly to Luka and put Damon in his arms to help him. The others came closer to hear Sai repeat Derek's message and to tell him he is sorry for being caught and leading them to Damon and the others. He also told them the royal family had had a problem with Damon's brother and told me that the prince was betrayed and sold to people that would harm him. Then he disappeared at the age of five from his captures and that is when they found him again. He was adopted my Derek's family.

"No need to apologize, my friend, you got him here in time. See he is already calmed down and resting. He really worries about all of us and he really does things we would think can't be done, yet here he is protecting us when we doubt him at times," Luka said.

Yuki walked forward and put his hand on Damon and said, "I was wrong Damon, please forgive me for not thinking and, Luka, I am sorry for pushing him and saying all I did."

"We can discuss this once he is rested and we can all sit down and talk," Luka stated.

With that he turned from his men and carried Damon to their room. Once inside he put Damon on the bed and went to the bathroom and turned on the water so the bath tube could fill with warm water.

As the water started to rise Luka went to the bed where Damon laid and began to undress him. Damon began to wake up just as he took off the last piece of clothing.

"You're covered in blood and dirt and I just wanted to wash you off so you can rest more comfortably," Luka said quietly.

Damon just smiled as Luka picked him up and carried him to the tube. Once Luka lowered him into the water, Damon sighed in relief as the water covered his body. Luka watched as all of Damon's stress and tenseness left his body.

Luka undressed himself then went from the bathroom and returned with clothes and towels. Luka gently leaned Damon forward and climbed into the massive bath with him and leaned Damon back on his chest while he began to wash him. As he finished cleaning himself and Damon, Luka refilled the tube with clean water and turned on the jets to help them relax some more in the hot water. After they relaxed and got unwound, Luka got out of the tube, dried off and got dressed then helped Damon

Once they were done in the bathroom they both walked out to join the others. Luka looked at Damon and asked if he was injured while he was gone? When Damon didn't reply off hand and just said if he was then Luka would have seen it during the bath. That's when Luka spun Damon around so his back faced him and saw a spot on his shoulder blade.

"I don't remember getting hurt by anything unless it was when I fell from the pain," Damon said.

"There is something there in the small cut but it's deep. I'll need help getting it out because it will hurt and you'll try to move."

Once they got to the others Luka looked at the men and asked them to make a place for Damon to lie down so he could get something from his back. He said they'll have to hold him still, so he wouldn't make the object go deeper. Luka got the first aid kit and got stuff out. As he had Damon lie down he sat on his back while the others held his arms and legs. As Luka began to dig that object out of Damon's back, Damon cried out in pain. As Luka pulled the object, all of them noticed just what it was when it was completely out.

"Why in the world would he have a stake and tracker in his back?" Sebastian asked.

"I don't know but it looks like it's been in there for a long time. So wherever this thing came from, there is a way to trace it back," Jaxon said.

Luka told Damon he was going to bandage him up but they all saw the blue flames heal his back.

"Well, it looks like we don't need to," Yuki said while smiling

When Damon didn't say anything to them, they laughed when they saw he had fallen asleep from the pain. When all of the men stood in a circle around him, they all dropped to their knees while Damon began to float. All of men ripped off their shirts and began to see symbols burning into their skin, and began to feel a connection to each other and most importantly they felt Damon. When the flames died out the men saw the symbols on them and the symbol that completely covered Luka.

"Damn, that fucking hurt," Sebastian said.

"Hurt would be an understatement to how that felt," Sai commented.

"However, it felt we have been chosen by Damon," Yuki said all serious like.

All too suddenly a sound came from the front of the house. They all shot up from the floor and then they were shocked.

"Holy shit, we're in the sunlight and we're not burning. How is this even possible?" Yuki asked.

Before anyone could reply, they were interrupted by the noise getting closer to the house. They all reacted just as the front door opened and Derek came in saying they had to hide Damon because his brother and his guards were coming to kill him.

"What the hell do you mean?" Luka asked.

"I found out long ago that Damon's brother had betrayed them all and tried to kill Damon for the throne," Derek answered.

"But, I thought the oldest son gets the crown next in line no matter what," Jaxon says.

"Yes that is the way of the royals, but Damon's brother is evil and will stop at nothing to get what he wants. That's why they hid Damon from everyone and when he began to have visions or dreams I was to take him to my family home for them to cover his memory with a life or a normal person until the time came for him to take his father's place."

"Why would you do such a thing to him? Why would you hide the very person he is and all that he could be?"

"It was the only way for his family to hide him among us wolves by masking what he is and make him to be a normal human to his brother."

"So why is he coming after him if he doesn't know he lives?"

"He knew Damon was alive as soon as the symbols burnt into his skin."

"What does that mean?" Sai asked.

"It means that the royals are bound together by their symbols and when one inherits them they all feel it. They don't go through what Damon does but their symbols turn blue as his turn red."

"And how would he find Damon exactly?"

"All royals can find each other if they are close to each other, so we have to keep them apart."

"And you came over here and told us we had to leave because his brother is close to finding Damon?"

"Yes, as my pack and I were leaving, my betas mate ran into him at the store and he asked if any of local pack members had seen him. He even had her call us to fund out. When I talked to him he was about three hours away. It took us an hour to get back to you guys and my whole pack is on the way to us. We are all going to my home so both packs can unite under me, and for my father to finally step down and be with my mother, and not worry about pack duties."

"And you're telling us this why exactly?"

"Because I am inviting you all to join us there and to keep Damon safe from being found and killed."

"How would he be kept safe? You just told us he would be found once they are in the same area," Jaxon snapped.

"Because nobody can get to my pack without being invited by the alpha or his family. We have a barrier that keeps everything out and everyone safe inside."

"Are you for real? His brother is a royal and nothing can keep out a royal, so I do think he'll be safe there."

"The king and queen couldn't even come into my home with him. They were frozen in place until they were invited in by my father, so yes it will keep him out."

"Okay we keep saying his brother or Damon's brother. What is his name?" Conrad asked.

"His name is Raven and his lackeys are Zero, Z, Conner, and the closest to him is Ceil. I have grown up with Damon, and I have kept him safe from any and all danger, pain, fear, loneliness, and dried all his tears when he wanted to remember where he came from. I sat up with him when he had nightmares and now I want to stay by his side because he is my brother and my best friend, and it is my job to keep him safe even if you guys are his royal guards. I am his family," Derek answered.

"But what about your pack? Wont they be angry that you brought us along. They don't really like royals and their guards do they?" Yuki asked.

"No they don't like them but they love Damon. He is part of the pack. No matter if he is royal or not, they know Damon will protect them as he always has protected me from making stupid choices in my life, and not keeping me to my promise to take over when my father needed me to and to join the packs together and make us a stronger stable family," Derek answered.

"I am sorry I cause you all so much pain. I am sorry I burden you guys so much. I will fix it. I promise you guys I won't be a problem anymore," Damon said then walked back into the room and shut the door.

"He thinks we all feel that he's a burden to us? After he saved our lives and chose us to be his guards, he thinks he is a burden to us?" Sebastian said sadly.

They all looked at each other and Luka was about to speak when Damon screamed. Luka and his men grabbed their symbols, looked at each other and saw they were glowing red; then they all ran to Damon's room and busted the door down.

They saw three men holding Damon and the other two had a knife at his throat. Raven was smiling at him.

"Dear brother, I finally found you. Mother and father will be so pleased to know you're alive, but you won't be for long. I plan on taking them your head," Raven said.

Before anyone could think of a plan, a pack mate jumped the guys who had Damon and shocked everyone by getting him free. He shoved Damon to Luka and those at the bedroom door and told them to run. Derek was about to join his pack mate in the fight but was frozen in his place, and could only watch as Raven and his guards ripped him apart. Damon grabbed Derek's arm and pulled him with them to leave. They all got out of the house. Luka picked up Damon while Derek's beta got Derek on his back and they all took off down the road to some car that was sitting not that far away. They all got into the cars and left in a big hurry.

"Where did these cars come from? They weren't here a little bit ago when I brought Damon back," Sai said.

"My men and I can't run at a blur and we can't cross the state in our wolf form so we used our cars," Derek answered with a smirk.

"That sounds logical but how in the world can these cars out run a vampire and his gang of wolves plus one hybrid?" Conrad asked.

"I don't know but it's a chance we have to take and see how well it helps," Luka said.

They traveled for a good long while and finally got to the state crossing. They pulled up and paid their way through and kept on driving. When they were far enough away, they pulled off the road and parked their cars at an abandoned house.

"We go on foot from here," Derek said.

They all got out and started heading for a passage way when they got surrounded by more people in cloaks.

CHAPTER 5

"No need to fear me. I will not hurt my twin brother," A man said as he pulled down his hood revealing who he is.

"Prince Demetri, what are you doing way out here?" Luka asked.

"I have been looking for my brother and now that I found him, he will be coming home with me. I refuse to let the wolves keep him any longer. It has taken me years to find him and I will not lose him again," Demetri said.

The people with Demetri surrounded Luka and the others and one man walked up and took Damon out of Luka's arms and took him to Demetri.

Damon woke up in Demetri's arms but instead of being afraid, he wrapped his arms around his brother and cried.

'"If you all want to continue living then you

will all follow me and my men," Demetri said

They all followed Demetri and his men into a cave and down a tunnel that led to a staircase.

"Where does this lead?" Luka asked.

"It leads somewhere you won't be able to find if you leave on your own. Only the twins know about this location, and they are the only ones who have ever been able to come and go as they please. Everyone else will only get lost in its maze," Demetri's guard said.

"Who are you people? I mean we know who he is but who are you guys?" Sai asked.

"We are Demetri's guards. My name is Leo and they are Sasuke, Raizo, Ran, Goemon and Demetri's right hand Hanzo. We are his guardians and you guys are just stand-in guardians until Damon meets his real guardians who have all been picked since birth. So if I were you all, I would take my leave now because you won't be wanted when he has his real guardians," Leo said.

"Guardian or not we won't be leaving his side until he himself tells us to. So thank you but I think we will wait to see what he says and see if he wants us to leave. The choice is his and his alone," Sebastian said.

"Leo, leave them be. They are right, it is Damon's choice if they stay or go so do not interfere with it. We all know what will happen, so let them find out for themselves," Hanzo said.

"But, Hanzo, they will get in the way of things and they will not let Damon go no matter what he says. They are vampires and everybody knows that once a vampire says they will stay with you forever they will literally never leave until either you or they die. A vampire is always true to their words. That is why I am saying this now instead of later," Leo argued.

"Leo, Hanzo, that is enough. Do not speak another word to them again unless it is in a civil manner. They have protected my brother and I am thankful for them. You will treat them right from now on. This is an order. Do you understand what I just said?" Demetri yelled at them.

"Yes, my prince, we understand," Hanzo and Leo said together.

They all walked up the stairs a little longer until they came to a door. When Demetri opened it they were stunned to see what was inside. They noticed three others there waiting.

"Demetri, you ran away before we could follow you and, well, we didn't want to get lost trying to find our way back to this place," Estal said.

"Hey Demetri who is that?" Chezem said.

"Don't you recognize Damon?"Demetri said.

The three of them looked so shocked they couldn't even form words. When Damon started to wake up, Demetri had sat him down in a chair so he would be able to see everyone around him, and Demetri could talk to him better while holding him.

"Who are you?" Damon asked with fear in his voice.

"I am your twin brother, Demetri, and I have been searching my whole life to find you after the wolves took you away from us when we were just children. I am so very happy I finally found you and I will never let you go again. I am so sorry I couldn't protect you when we were little and I couldn't stop them from taking you away from us," Demetri said sadly.

"I feel like I am connected to you and you don't scare me, but who are those three? They scare me," Damon said.

"No need to fear us, Damon, we were all raised together. But, my name is Estal and I am an elf. This is Chezem and he is a demon. This is Kotaro and he is a fairy. We all have been friends for a very long time and even though you have been gone we are all still friends. We will never hurt you or leave you. We are all sorry that we couldn't save you when you were taken and we will make it up to you by never leaving your side again. We will all protect you from now on if you are willing to put up with us being clingy to each other again. We are all very happy to have you back home with us again," Estal said while crying happy tears.

"Um….. ok," Damon said.

Just then three of the vampires yelled in pain just as Chezem, Estal and Kotaro dropped to their knees in pain. Damon saw that his mark now rested on the three new guardians while another mark appeared on the three vampires.

"What does that mark mean?" Damon asked.

"It would seem you now have a start on your royal guards. The ones who will follow you everywhere you go and nobody can get past them," Demetri answered.

"But I thought that is what the guardians are for. Why do I need a royal guard?" Damon asked.

"Yes that is what the guardians are for, but

some of us royalty have to have a royal guard just in case the guardians are busy with us. The guards will move throughout the castle while the guardians remain by our sides, and when things get sticky, they all come to guard us so none of them will fall in battle." Demetri said.

Damon looked around at all of them and then at Demetri, and when their eyes met, he started to cry. Demetri wrapped his arms around Damon and held him while he cried.

"Why is this happening to me? What did I ever do to go through all of this?" Damon asked.

"I am sorry, dear brother, but, know this, it will not happen again. You are now safe with me and nothing will ever get to you again. I swear it," Demetri said.

The boys sat in the chair for a while before they both fell asleep. Hanzo and Chezem walked over and they each picked up a boy and took them over to the bed so they could sleep comfortably and not be cramped in a chair.

"I could have moved Damon, Chezem. He is not used to you touching him and I don't want him freaking out and hurting someone," Luka said.

"That's funny, but I know more about that boy than you will ever know. Yes I know about his flames and the fact they hurt him whenever it covers his body. Just so you know, his flames have never hurt any of us. Do you know why that is? No, then let me tell you. He has never hurt us because we are all bound to each other by blood and the boys control each other's flames. If one is set ablaze, then put the other next to him because they are each other's trigger. And let me worn you if you touch or take Damon away from Demetri without his approval, you will all burn. So it was best for me to move him and not you because with the bond we share, he knew it was me around him and not an outsider," Chezem said.

"Do you have a mark?" Jaxon asked.

The three of them revealed their wrist that held the band markings that went all the way up to their elbows. It had symbols that showed their initials and they were intertwined together and they were bonded to each other far deeper than any other bond. That's when Luka and they all knew they couldn't do anything to keep them apart from each other.

Not long after the boys fell asleep, Damon's body erupted with blue flames and he was screaming in pain. Demetri shot up out of bed and the other three joined him. When Luka approached, Demetri ignited with his flames and tried to burn Luka, but Hanzo jumped in front of him and pushed him away from the boys and the others. Once Demetri put his arms around Damon, they both began to calm down and fall back into a peaceful sleep. The others walked over to Luka and his men.

"Did I not tell you if you try to get close you will be burnt? Demetri does not know you and I don't think he will be that accepting of you as the wolves are, but you will need to be patient and let him be the one to clue you in. Now you and the wolves go over there and wait until we tell you it is safe for you all to move around. I do not want Damon to wake up and find out he killed someone when we can keep that from happening. Now please go over there and wait," Chezem said.

Luka and the others walked over to the sitting area away from the boys so the others could work on getting them to put out their fires and to keep them from hurting somebody. It took a couple of hours before they finally got the boys to settle down and rest peacefully.

Hanzo and Chezem walked over to the guys in the sitting area and began telling them what had to take place if they were going to stay around.

"In order for you all to remain here you must do as we tell you or it can be fatal for you. As you saw if any of you try to touch or move Damon away from Demetri you will surely die. They have both suffered enough, and there is no need to separate them any longer than what they have been. So please do not try to take him away from him," Chezem said.

"We will let you know when it is safe for you to be around him and when you can be around him and when you can do things, but for right now just tread on thin ice when you're around them," Hanzo says.

The others looked at each other, then at Hanzo and Chezem as Luka spoke

"We have kept him safe from harm and we also brought him to you. Now you're saying we have to tread on thin ice when none of us would ever harm Damon or his brother," Luka said.

"That may be true but as of right now Demetri doesn't see it that way. With as close as you all are to Damon, he feels that at any time you will take him away and try to keep him away just to protect him. Demetri feels threatened by that and we want to show him it won't happen by taking it slow in having you guys around," Chezem replied.

They all just looked at each other until there was screaming coming from the bed. They looked over and saw Demetri holding Damon down and blue flames erupting as Damon screamed in pain.

"What is happening to him?" Demetri asked as he looked at the vampires.

"Let me come to him please. I can help. For some reason when I touch him, the dreams disappear and he can rest easy," Luka answered.

"Then come," Demetri ordered.

They all watched as Luka walked over to Damon. When Luka held Damon's hand they all saw him relax and sleep easier and the flames died down.

"What are these dreams he has been having?" Demetri asked.

"I don't really know but, when he has them, he always has a fresh bite mark on his neck from them. It takes days for them to heal and we also found a tracking device in his back in the form of a stake. When we pulled it out, it was like it has been there for years, like someone was keeping tabs on him or someone was keeping track of where he is always at," Luka answered.

"I have a picture of it," Jaxon said and then almost jumped out of his skin as Demetri appeared by him in a flash.

"Show me," he said.

Jaxon showed Demetri the photo and they all

watched as Demetri's expression changed.

"He had that in his back?" Demetri gasped.

"Yes he did and it was a nightmare trying to pull it out" Luka said.

"Hanzo, I want you to send a messenger to the castle and tell our parents that Raven is the one who has known all along where Damon was, and he is the one trying to kill him and take the throne for himself; and add that we will be returning to the castle in a few days and have the guards double to keep us safe," Demetri ordered.

"Yes, sir," Hanzo said then went to send a messenger with a note to the castle for his prince.

Once the message was sent, Hanzo noticed someone leave the room, so he and a few others followed the strange acting guy.

"Sir, they sent a messenger to the castle. I'm trying to follow him to tell you which direction he is going," The man said then hung up a phone.

"You will not be telling him anything, but you will be telling us everything," Hanzo said as the other two grabbed the man.

They all walked back to the others and when they entered the room everybody looked at Hanzo and Derek step forward and demand to know why one of his men was in the arms of his two guards.

"This man is sending information to someone within Raven's group and is giving him information on the Princes, so if you want to join your pack mate you will make him tell us everything he knows," Hanzo snapped.

"Jonas, is that true?" Derek asked.

"Yes I have been sending information to Raven

because he said he could get me from under your command and he would help me become free of the pack and never have to answer to anyone again," Jonas said.

CHAPTER 6

"Jonas, if you do that then you will be killed because there isn't any way to become free of the pack or to become free of my rule because I am the king of the wolves and whatever I say goes. That includes those who don't wish to be controlled and, also, if you did become free you would have to either join a pack or be killed for betraying us. Those are you choices and if I were you I would tell us everything you know and then kill yourself, because once you are done telling us what we want to know, you will be put to the death in front of the whole pack," Derek said.

Jonas began to tell them everything Raven had told him. That he would be able to be free of all the wolves if his job was successful and he would be able to rule with him and be in command of a grand army.

"You are a fool for believing him and thinking he would give you any part of ruling over something. You are nothing but a pawn to him and he will kill you once he has everything he wants. So I guess you lose your life for something that was never in your favor to begin with. You also lose your family over something that would have cost us all dearly," Derek said.

They all looked at Jonas and then they heard someone talking.

"He is lying. He is in with Raven so that he has the chance to kill you and take over the wolf world while Raven takes over the others. Then together they will go after the humans and enslave them and have them for their personal amusement. Then and only then they will both get what they want," Damon said.

Jonas looked at Damon shocked but he said nothing, and then tried to launch himself at Damon. "You will die by my hands and not Raven's and once our plan is done, I will kill Raven and rule over everybody, and have my own personal fun killing everyone that goes against me," Jonas shouted but in the next instant he burst into flames.

"You will not touch my brother and you will die right now by my hands for your lack of information. You see I am Damon's twin and I control flames just as he does, but my flames kill those who try to harm him or me and his flames heal the injured and give them a gift of being in the sunlight or being able to do my rule because I am the king of the wolves and whatever I say goes. That includes those who don't wish to be controlled and, also, if you did become free you would have to either join a pack or be killed for betraying us. Those are you choices and if I were you I would tell us everything you know and then kill yourself, because once you are done telling us what we want to know, you will be put to the death in front of the whole pack," Derek sent for four more people, and they all were put to death by Demetri's flames in front of everybody and then Demetri spoke.

"Anybody else want to betray us and try to hide it? No? Then I suggest you all start packing things up because we are leaving for the castle as soon as you are finished." Demetri said angrily.

Everybody went about their packing while the others went to wait for everything to be done, and once everything was packed they set off for the castle. They walked out of the secret tunnels and towards their cars and loaded everything up and began their journey home.

They went through several states and saw some awesome sights but the one sight they were happy to see was the castle that sat in the middle of a never ending forest. They also saw some of the wolves that guard the castle and every other thing that was outside in their care.

When they pulled up and parked their car, they got out and walked up to the door only to be met by two people. Damon stood frozen as Demetri ran up and hugged them both and called them mom and dad.

"Damon, don't be afraid. This is our mom and dad and they have been missing you just as much as I have and they would be happy to hug you,"

Demetri said.

"I'm sorry but I'm not really ready to accept things just yet. I have been without them for a while. Please, just let me figure things out first," Damon said as he hid behind Luka and the others.

"Damon, I am sorry. I shouldn't push you. Please forgive me. I don't want you upset with me and I am upsetting you and pushing you to accept things. We will take it slow. Mom and dad understand that this is a lot for you to take in and accept all at once," Demetri said sadly.

Damon stepped out from behind Luka and smiled at Demetri. Demetri smiled back and walked up to Damon and grabbed him up into a hug and said he would always protect his smile and promised to never let him be alone again.

The next instant there was an explosion and the brothers flew apart. Raven stood in between them and smiled as two of his men grabbed Damon and ran off with him.

"Now, little brother, I will have things my way or you will never see him again. Farewell for now." Raven laughed as he got away.

"Damon…..Damon……DAMON!!!!!!!!!!!!!!" Demetri yelled as his anger began to take over.

Demetri was so angry that if anyone got close to him he started burning everyone, then he saw the wolves bringing someone to them. He ran over and grabbed the man and asked him where Raven was taking his brother and if he lied he would be burnt bit by bit until he told the truth, but the guy just said he was taking him back to his apartment and making it seem like everything was nothing but a dream; because Raven planned on giving him serum that would wipe his mind from everything and he would be the only one to teach him things and make it seem like they have always been together. That Raven was going to make Damon his little puppet.

Demetri did not like this news and he burnt the man to a crisp, then turned to Derek and told him to take him to where they lived before they set out to keep Damon safe. What they didn't know was that Damon had gotten out of the hold of the two men who dragged him off and was running lost in the woods, until a wolf came up to him and stopped him. The wolf went behind a tree and changed into a man, then stepped out and came over to Damon.

"Do not fear me. I will call and tell the others you are safe from Raven, but you must follow me to hide. I can cover your scent so they can't follow it to the hide out. Now please follow me," The man said.

They walked for a bit before coming up to a cabin and once inside, the man called the castle and told them of Damon's safety and that the prince would be showing up shortly because he is so angry he wants to see if it was true or not that Damon was safe with him. When he hung up the phone, Damon walked over to the couch and sat down. Not long after he fell asleep. The man covered him with a blanket just as Demetri stormed through the door and stopped when he saw Damon sleeping on the couch. He then dropped to his knees in front of him and laid his head on his lap then fell asleep himself. When Damon woke up he saw Demetri sitting in front of him with his head on his lap. Damon pushed hair out of Demetri's face and saw that his eyes had opened up, Then Demetri stood and laid on the couch and put his head in his brother's lap and smiled up at him.

"I let him get his hands on you for a second time. I am very sorry." Demetri said sadly.

"It is alright. I got away and this man found me and brought me here. I guess I fell asleep and woke up to you sleeping with your head on my lap. I didn't mean to wake you up. When I moved your hair out of your face I just wanted to make sure it was really you," Damon replied.

"Yes it is me, dear brother, and I will not let you go. I will find a way to keep you safe, and I will find a way to stop Raven from harming you and wiping your memories of all of us. I will never let you forget me or our family. But, we will be going somewhere far away so that he won't be able to find you. And I hope everything will work in our favor with this," Demetri told him.

"Where are we going?" Damon asked.

"We are going to go stay with our vampire and Elvin friends in the forest across from ours. Raven never goes there because he never really cares for them, and he knows we would never go there so he wouldn't think to look there. It was Chezem and Lukas idea to do this in the first place," Demetri answered.

"Sir, I am sorry to interrupt you, but we must move now. My men have told me that Raven and his men are searching the forest for Damon," The man said.

"Thank you. Please have your pack surround us

and cover our scent while we walk to the forest. Then after we are safe, return to the castle and protect our parents," Demetri said.

They walked out of the cabin and were surrounded by the pack. They began to walk to the spot where the two forests join together and once they got there they would be surrounded by vampires and elves for protection until they got safely into the castle with the kings and queens. It took them about an hour to reach the spot, then they switched guards as the wolves ran off to go protect their parents as the brothers went the other way for their own safety.

It was night by the time they reached the Elvin castle and they saw that both kings and queens where standing there waiting for their arrival. When they got to the top of the steps, the kings and queens bowed to them and stepped to the side as they entered the castle.

"Why are the bowing to us? Aren't they the rulers over this kingdom?" Damon asked.

"Yes but we are higher ranking then them. We are their rulers and they must protect us or every race will die," Demetri said.

When they got to the throne room the Elvin king told the princes to sit on the thrones. Damon didn't really want to sit on the throne because he still wasn't sure about any of this and was still trying to accept that he had a family and someone trying to kill him, and it was his older brother who was the one behind everything that is happening because he wanted the throne but couldn't have it because he only showed a vampire trait instead of all of them like him and his twin.

The boys just looked around, then walked up to the throne and sat down and noticed that several people started coming into the throne room and bowing down to them.

"My princes it is an honor to have you both in our kingdoms, these are our fine warriors and are willing to protect you both with their lives if need be. We have trained long and hard for you and we will keep you both safe from any harm that is to come our way. Please rest easy and know that you are safe," The Elvin king said.

"Um…. I am sorry but might I know your name?" Damon asked.

"Of course I am sorry. My name is Lucas and this is Violet and here we have Ruby and Maxwell. Forgive me for not introducing ourselves sooner," Lucas said as he bowed.

"No need to be sorry I am the one who should be. I was taken when I was little and I can't really remember anybody's names," Damon said sadly.

Demetri got up and wrapped his arms around his brother as he started to cry.

Everyone stood there in shock after learning that about the prince. Then they started to get mad because someone took him from his family and he has been without them for so long that he is learning everything. It made them all sad for him because of all he has suffered and they felt bad because everything is all new to him and it is taking its toll on him.

Demetri picked up Damon and held him while he cried until he fell asleep in his arms. Then the king told him their rooms were ready for them. Demetri carried his brother to their room and laid him on the bed and then laid down next to him. The king said that there were several guards throughout the hall and there would be a few of them within the room with them for their safety. Demetri just nodded then fell asleep with his brother still in his arms.

Demetri was awoken by someone walking in the room so when he covered both him and Damon in his flames an elf walked over to them and asked if all was well. Demetri just smiled and said he forgot there were guards in the room with them and he fell back asleep while keeping his flames covering them.

The next morning Damon woke up to his brother still sleeping, so he got up and went to take a shower. When he returned, his and his brother's guards were in the room and some of them were injured, so Damon ran over and began to heal them with his flames but as he was doing it the wounds that were on them began to show up on Damon. As they showed up on him, his blue flame closed them quickly and when he came to the man who was extremely hurt, he felt Demetri put his hand on his shoulder. Then Damon healed the man and the wound showed on Damon, but Demetri's flame healed it with Damon's blue flame because it was bad, but everyone was all healed and Damon had to take yet another shower. When he was done this time he saw someone had brought them food. He was told it was safe to eat because it was all checked and it was safe to eat and drink.

When they were done, they all walked to the throne room so they could all come up with a plan to take out their brother, so they could all live in peace with each other and be able to rule and keep their world safe from any and all kinds of harm.

When they stepped into the throne room, both of the brothers froze as the saw Estal and Chezem talking to the king about things they could do to keep the princes safe. When they saw the boys they couldn't look away from them so they both just started walking over to the boys and wrapped them both in their arms and said they would forever stay by their sides and never let them be hurt or let anything hurt them. Then they pulled away and then kissed them like they couldn't believe. Once they pulled apart, the Elvin king and the whole court rejoiced as the king announced that the princes have found their soul mates and that the kingdoms will forever be united and would always stand by each other's sides.

So, the kings and queens set forth to begin the festivities of the joining of the Elvin and Fairy world, with the royal court of the high royalty of the supernatural world. They sent word out to all the surrounding kingdoms and to the boys' parents about the joining and the celebration would begin for them in a week's time.

Who knows when Raven would show up or what would he plan to do? Nobody was thinking of that because they have to celebrate the four people who found out they were each other's soul mate. But what do you think will happen if Raven finds his in the most shocking way. Would he keep his mate or will he not even accept his mate and keep things the way they are…Who knows?

Find out in Raven's mate.

EPILOGUE

When Raven would show up or what would he plan to do? Nobody was thinking of that because they have to celebrate the four people who found out they were each other's soul mate. But what do you think will happen if Raven finds his in the most shocking way. Would he keep his mate or will he not even accept his mate and keep things the way they are…Who knows?

COMING SOON: Raven's mate.

.

ABOUT THE AUTHOR

Jessica was raised on a 'big rig' and lived in many places. In her younger years she wrote poetry, but in her adult years, her mom talked her in spreading her creative wings. That's when Jessica started to writing short stories, novellas and novels.

Once she met and married her wonderful husband, they settled in the beautiful Ozarks and had two amazing children. Jessica's husband also encouraged her to write and pushed her to finish this story, but life got in the way and the writing was slow. She feared her publisher wouldn't understand, but was pleased that Paperback-Press stood beside her with encouragement and patience.

Now she's working on 'RAVEN'S MATE', the sequel to 'THE BETRAYED PRINCE'.

She enjoys writing and hopes you enjoy reading her work.